Akbar's India

Akbar's India

Growing Up and Becoming a Great Emperor

MARCIA THOMPSON

BALESTIER PRESS
LONDON · SINGAPORE

Balestier Press
Centurion House, London TW18 4AX
www.balestier.com

Akbar's India
Copyright © Marcia Thompson, 2019

First published by Balestier Press in 2019

Image credits:
Painting 1 (page 13), British Library, London;
Painting 2 (page 17), Fitzwilliam Museum, Cambridge, England;
Painting 3 (page 21), Victoria and Albert Museum, London;
Painting 4 (page 25), Victoria and Albert Museum, London;
Painting 5 (page 29), Victoria and Albert Museum, London;
Painting 6 (page 33), Victoria and Albert Museum, London;
Painting 7 (page 37), Chester Beatty Library, Dublin;
Painting 8 (page 41), Aga Khan Museum, Toronto.

A CIP catalogue record for this book
is available from the British Library.

ISBN 978 1 911221 25 8

For Helen Wang

Kevin and Aidan

Content

A cheetah at Akbar's court

A Book for Exploring

This book is not just for reading; it is a book for exploring. What you have are copies of eight paintings made during Akbar's lifetime (1542-1605) and under his direction to tell the story of his life. By just looking at the paintings you can get some idea of what life at the time was like for him and what was important to him.

The writing for each chapter explains what is happening in the miniature that follows on the next page and you will need to keep turning back and forth to keep up.

The circular cut-outs opposite the painting in each chapter show people or things that are particularly important to the story and are set out for you to match to the painting.

At the bottom of the page there is a list of very small tricky details for you to find in the painting. There is a key at the end of the book which will tell you if you got this right.

The second section of the book is for the truly curious. It repeats the cut-outs and gives a background story for each. It tells you more about the amazing Akbar and his times.

The writing in the book is based on the records that Akbar kept, so by reading this you can go back to the pictures and see even more in them. This book can help you see Akbar as Akbar saw himself.

1

A Difficult Beginning

Akbar's babyhood and separation from his parents

Akbar became a very rich and powerful ruler of a great Muslim empire called the Mughal Empire, but his life did not begin well. When it came time for him to be born his mother and father were crossing a desert with a small army of soldiers. It was the hottest time of the year and the sun beat down on them day after day. There was very little water and many of their horses and camels died. Finally they reached a small town called Umarkot and this is where Akbar was born.

Akbar's father, Humayun, had been driven from his kingdom in India by an enemy and he was travelling about trying to raise a big enough army to fight his way back. He was not at Umarkot when Akbar was born because he had moved on to a campsite to be with his soldiers. When a messenger arrived to tell him of Akbar's birth, he was very happy but embarrassed because he was too poor to give out presents to celebrate the birth. Instead he took a container of musk (perfume) and broke it open. As the scent from the musk filled the tent he said he hoped his son's fame would spread through all the world as the scent was spreading through their tent. This is exactly what happened, but it certainly did not look very likely at the time.

When Akbar was six months old he travelled with his mother to join his father in the camp and they were together for a short time, but when he was a year and three months old his father and mother decided to make a trip to Persia to ask for soldiers from the Shah of Persia. It was a very difficult trip across deserts and over mountains, too dangerous for a small baby, so they had to leave him behind. He was cared for by his nurse and by relatives who lived in the nearby cities of Qandahar and Kabul.

The Shah of Persia agreed to give an army of soldiers to Akbar's father, but it took a long time and Akbar did not see his parents again until he was three years old. By this time, his nurse had taken him to Kabul. Akbar's relatives were curious to know if Akbar would recognise his mother. They put him on a couch near the entrance of the room. Akbar's mother entered in a crowd of other women. Akbar picked her out and immediately ran to her. In the miniature on the next page he is seated on her lap while a great party is held to celebrate the reunion of the family.

Akbar's father, Humayun

Akbar and his mother

Mughal carpets

A drummer

A dancer

Refreshments

Wall painting

Can you also find?

Two swords.

A fly whisk.

A dagger.

A forest of trees.

Three containers of drinks.

Two horn players.

Two minarets.

2

Growing Up

Successes and failures in Akbar's early life

Akbar grew up in Kabul. He was a very active boy as you can see in the miniature where he is hunting with his friends. He was a good shot with a bow and arrow and could fire a gun. He liked to race on the back of a camel at great speeds. He enjoyed the royal pigeons as they had been trained to do amazing tricks. When he blew a whistle in one way they would all fly together in rhythm. For another command, they would dance or do somersaults in the air.

He was interested in all sorts of sports, in particular wrestling. When he and his cousin got into an argument about a brightly painted kettle drum, his uncle suggested that they have a wrestling match to decide the matter. Akbar easily threw his cousin at the very beginning of the match, even though the cousin was older and bigger.

Sitting on the sidelines and watching was not something Akbar ever wanted to do. Once when he was given a pair of oxen as a present, he insisted on taking the reins in his hands and driving the oxen about near his home, even though it was very much against the custom of the times for royal princes to do anything associated with manual labour.

Great care was taken with Akbar's education. Humayun, Akbar's father, employed two famous Persian painters to teach Akbar art. He showed his work to his father from time to time and his father was pleased with his progress.

There was one thing, however, that Akbar never learned to do—he never learned to read and write. He and his first tutor spent most of their time playing with the pigeons. When his father heard about this he found another tutor for Akbar, but this tutor was no more successful. In the end, Akbar had four tutors in succession, but he never got as far as learning his letters. Sometimes he would run and hide in order to avoid lessons.

No one knows why Akbar refused to learn his letters. In his time all royal princes and princesses learned to read. His father was a great reader who always had a large library of books in any place he lived and a camel loaded with books following him when he travelled. His father talked to him about it and when he was away sent letters urging him to try. He even sent some of his own poetry, thinking that this might get him started, but nothing worked. At the end of his life Akbar could neither read nor write.

Akbar hunting

A falconer

Falcon with prey

Water for the hunters

A young archer

Two deer

A royal servant

Can you also find?

Two swords.

Two birds on a rock.

Four birds in flight.

Yak tail decoration for a horse.

A pink flower.

3

The Teenage Emperor

Akbar's ascension to emperor and rebellious teenage years

Akbar was twelve years old when his father, Humayun, decided it was time to go to war and get back the territory he had lost in India. Akbar fought in his father's army and they managed to gain back some of this land.

Once they were settled into a new life in India his father gave him an advisor, Bairam Khan, and sent him to rule over a province in the empire. Akbar hadn't been there very long when word came that his father had died in an accident. He had heard the call to prayer and was coming down the stairs from his library when he tripped on his robe and fell over the side of the stairs. He died two days later.

The death of Humayun made Akbar an emperor at the age of thirteen. This was a very dangerous position for him because his father had many rivals, and when they heard that a thirteen year old boy was on the throne, they began to make plans to take the empire away from him. Bairam Khan helped him fight to keep what he had inherited from his father. Their biggest battle was fought near Delhi against an enemy with a huge contingent of elephants carrying knives and spears in their trunks. Just when it looked as though the enemy might win, their commander was shot through the eye with an arrow. The arrow pierced his brain and he slumped over on his elephant. When his soldiers saw this, they completely gave up and ran away in confusion.

Bairam Khan helped Akbar fight other battles, and Akbar was very dependent on him to keep the empire he had gained and to rule it. But during this time Akbar, to many people, did not seem to be very concerned. He appeared to be a typical teenager, interested mainly in sports and games. He was fond of polo and spent many hours playing the game with his friends. He became skilled in working with elephants and on more than one occasion when an elephant had gone wild he quickly scrambled up a wall or a tree nearby and as the runaway elephant thundered past he jumped down onto its back and brought it under control.

In the miniature you can see Akbar on his elephant, Sky Rocket, chasing a runaway elephant across a bridge supported only by boats. Everyone is worried and people are jumping into the river in order to save him in case he fell.

Akbar on Sky Rocket

Lifted boats

An argument

The ferryman

A royal servant

Gardeners

A garden house

Can you also find?

Eight bells.

A jumping fish.

A black feather.

Five cypress trees.

Two yak tail standards.

Two open viewing platforms.

4

Fighting for the Empire

Description of the battle for Ranthambor

At the age of eighteen Akbar decided to stop playing and to take charge of the empire himself. He convinced Bairam Khan to go on a trip to Mecca and leave the running of the country to him. Unfortunately, on the way Bairam was attacked and killed by someone who had a grudge against him.

During this early period in his reign Akbar spent most of his time fighting battles. When his father died he only controlled a small stretch of land in northern India. Akbar was determined to get back all the land that had once belonged to his family and to add new lands to his empire.

His soldiers respected him because he used all the energy he had once used in playing games to fight the enemy, sometimes face to face. He was tireless and would travel on horseback or by elephant at great speeds shocking the enemy by arriving sooner than expected. If necessary he would travel during the monsoon season in the pouring rain through forests or over fields with heavy mud underfoot.

The painting on the next page shows the siege of Ranthambor—a large fort that had been built on top of a very steep hill making it difficult for an enemy to attack. If they approached anywhere near the wall the people of the the city could fire at them with bows and arrows or just throw down rocks on their heads and make it impossible for them to get closer.

Akbar countered this by ordering underground tunnels built so that his soldiers could attack the walls of the city safely. He also ordered that a nearby hill be used as a battle station and with great difficulty had big guns dragged up the side of the hill by oxen and pointed at the walls of the city. The guns were very heavy and awkward and difficult to fire, but when they were fired they destroyed a section of the city wall and several buildings. The noise of the firing echoed through the surrounding countryside with a terrible roar and the people of the city very soon begged to surrender.

This was one kind of battle that Akbar fought called a siege, where an army surrounded a place and waited for the people inside to give up. It was not the main sort of battle that he fought. If you look closely at the painting you will see several soldiers with horses making their way into the city. This was Akbar's greatest strength. His army was mainly made up of soldiers who were brilliant horsemen and wonderful archers. Throughout his reign this support kept him in power and made it possible for him to enlarge his empire.

The use of force was not the only way Akbar built his empire. He often used diplomacy, meeting with kings and princes from different areas to convince them that they were better off cooperating with him than fighting against him. He sometimes married the daughters of kings as a peaceful way of gaining territory. This was possible because Muslim law at that time allowed a man to have more than one wife.

The big guns

The cavalry

The tent city

Entrance into the city

Rao Surjan Singh

A sword

The foot soldiers

Can you also find?

Eight bushes growing into the side of the hill.

A dagger.

Pita bread.

A yak tail horse decoration.

5

Making the Empire Work

Akbar's view of his obligations as emperor

At this point in our story it might seem right to call Akbar 'an action man' because of his great strength and daring, but this wouldn't be the whole truth. Akbar had another side to him; he was very thoughtful. He knew that it wasn't good enough just to conquer a country, he also had to make it work. The people had to be content with the way things were managed and the laws had to be fair to everyone. He worked very hard to make this happen.

When he wasn't fighting wars Akbar held court every day with the help of some of his nobles, the people who helped him run the empire. At the court session he and his nobles would discuss problems that had come up in the empire and how they could be solved. Ordinary people could come to this court and tell him about any wrongs they had suffered at the hands of his government officials. If Akbar was convinced they were telling the truth he would see that the official was punished and the matter was put right for the person complaining.

In the miniature he is talking to the four year old son of Bairam Khan after Bairam was killed on the way to Mecca. He is telling the little boy not to worry, that he will take care of him like a father.

It wasn't a totally serious court. People brought their pet animals because they knew Akbar liked animals. As you can see they also brought musical instruments. At the end of the court session singers, both men and women, performed and there were jugglers, comedians and acrobats.

People brought gifts to Akbar and he gave many gifts as well, some to his soldiers and some to the people who were helping rule the empire. He also gave presents to musicians and artists or to anyone doing a good and useful job like the people caring for his animals.

If Akbar was exceptionally pleased with someone he might give them a horse or an elephant or a beautifully decorated sword or dagger. He often gave away gold coins. On one occasion he gave a pond full of gold coins to a singer because he liked his music. Jewellery was a frequent present along with special clothing known as ceremonial robes.

Abd ur-Raham

Akbar's nobles

Vina player

A lute player

A royal horse

A pet cheetah

Red headed falcon

Can you also find?

A bull.

A fly whisk.

A sword.

Three daggers.

Two yak tail decorations.

A shield.

A white falcon.

6

Akbar's City

The building of Fatehpur Sikri

When Akbar took over his empire most of the land was countryside: farms, forests and empty open spaces. He felt that to have a wealthy empire it was necessary to have cities. He built cities himself and encouraged other people to build them and fill them with factories, shops and homes.

To celebrate the birth of his first son he built a city and named it Fatehpur Sikri. The city is still standing and is visited by thousands of people every year. There is a huge mosque with a courtyard where ten thousand people can worship and a palace where Akbar lived. The palace has an open courtyard where he met with people as described in the last chapter. There is a private section called a harem where he lived with his wives and his children. There are also buildings and open spaces for entertaining visitors. Akbar had a pond built with an island in the centre where poets, singers and dancers could perform. In the same courtyard a huge pachisi board was built into the stone pavings where he played the game with his friends.

The buildings were made of brick faced with red sandstone. The stone was decorated with many carvings. Both Hindu and Muslim designs were used because Akbar liked to mix styles. While the buildings were going up he was often out in the midst of the activity, talking to the workmen and sometimes pitching in and helping.

Once Akbar started building the mosque and his palace some of his nobles came to live here and a city grew up around the palace walls. A market with factories and shops soon developed. Akbar loved this market and often could be found here watching the work in the factories and sometimes getting involved himself. He especially enjoyed ribbon making and there were occasions when his nobles needed him for official matters and they found him here, happily making ribbons on a loom.

The city is located on the edge of an artificial lake that was fed by a local river and managed by a system of dams that stored the water in the rainy season and released it as it was needed. The lake was two miles long and a half a mile wide. On hot days cooling winds from the lake would blow across the city. There were gardens along the edge and when Akbar had a holiday he came here with his wives and children. At other times there were lakeside parties with many people playing games or watching sports events.

Carving a design

Splitting stone

A jali screen

An ox

Room in the harem

Making mortar

A porter

Can you also find?

Akbar's secretary with pen and paper.

Two falcons.

Green ceramic tiles.

A marble pool.

Two birds on a railing.

A tree on the side of a hill.

A keyhole doorway.

7

Akbar's Religion

Akbar's failure to unite the different religions in his empire into one religion

So far in our story of Akbar as an adult you have seen him go from one success to another. He did, however, have his failures. The most outstanding was his failure to change the attitude of the people in his empire to religion.

Akbar was a Muslim but he was very interested in other religions. The majority of the people living in the empire were Hindu. Akbar liked this religion and visited Hindu holy men to learn more about it. He invited other holy men to his palace and sometimes talked with them all night.

Akbar also liked a very old religion called Zoroastrianism which used the sun and fire in their worship to help people understand God. In sympathy with their ideas, Akbar included the worship of the sun in his daily prayers. In the evenings when the lamps in his palace were lit, he asked everyone to stand in respect for the fire.

Christian monks (Jesuits) came at Akbar's invitation to stay at his palace and teach him about the Christian religion. The monks built a chapel for their worship. Akbar visited their chapel and took off his turban to show his respect. His sons, when they came, were charmed by the pictures of Jesus as a baby.

Holy men from the Jain religion also came to see Akbar and tell him about their faith. One holy man, Hiravijaya Suri, lived in Gujarat, 800 km from Fatipur Sikri where Akbar was living. He walked the entire distance to speak with Akbar and in the end convinced him to let birds out of their cages and free people held in prisons.

It seemed to Akbar that all religions were good. He decided to bring together priests and teachers from the different faiths so they could discuss their beliefs and develop them into one religion that would satisfy everyone. He put up a special building in Fatipur Sikri for this gathering and called it the House of Worship. The miniature shows a meeting between Muslim clerics and Jesuit priests. On occasion Muslims, Hindus, Christians, Jains and Zoroastrians all came together to talk about their faiths. The project was a failure; they could not agree on anything. In the end Akbar gave up and had the building torn down.

Although Akbar failed in this, people today looking back to his time admire him for trying. In the modern world there are many who feel there is good in all religions and that people of different religions should not be fighting each other but finding a way to get on together.

Jesuit priests

Muslim clerics

Akbar

Akbar's son, Salim

Child in street

Muslim holy book

Money bags

Can you also find?

Thirteen books.

A loaf of bread.

A tree.

A dagger.

A yak tail.

8

The Workshop for Books

A description of the processes used to produce Akbar's many books

Although Akbar never learned to read and write, he loved books. At the end of his life he had a library of 24,000 books. He bought some of the books, but many of them were produced in workshops like the one shown in the miniature.

At the top of the painting two calligraphers (people with special writing skills) are working together. It appears that the older one is a master teaching the younger. If you look closely you can see that the young man has finished an entire page and seems to be waiting with his pen poised above the paper. He may be about to add the title, but is waiting for the master to tell him just how to do this.

Just below them an artist and a calligrapher are talking to each other. The artist is leaning forward eagerly. He seems anxious to understand the book they are working on so he can draw the pictures accurately. Behind them another young artist is working on the picture of a horse. Out in the garden a paper-maker is at work. He is rubbing the paper with a stone to make it smooth for the calligraphers and artists.

When Akbar's father came to India he brought with him the two artists from Persia, Mir Sayyid Ali and Abd al-Samad, who had been Akbar's art teachers when he was a boy. Other Persian artists made the long journey to India when they heard about the opportunities in Akbar's workshop. Persian artists were famous for the precision and elegance of their work. Akbar invited Indian artists to join his workshop. These artists added a brightness and liveliness to the pictures.

Looking at the painting, you can see that every effort was made to make the artists comfortable. They sit on beautiful carpets and there are two servants, one on each side of the building ready to serve them refreshment from the table just outside the room. While they work they look out on a garden with a flowering tree, channels for running water and a pond.

When Akbar had the time he spent hours every day listening while scholars read his books to him. He had an unusual ability to remember what he heard, so in spite of his failure to read and write, he became a person with a wide understanding of the world. This understanding made him one of India's greatest rulers because it enabled him to see and sympathise with the many different points of view held by the people he ruled.

Student of calligraphy

Teacher of calligraphy

Paper maker

Artist at work

Artist with horse drawing

Carved stone pillar

The drinks table

Can you also find?

Four carpets with red flowers.

An aqueduct.

Thirteen birds.

A pond.

A flowering cherry tree.

A channel of running water.

که او را قدرت استنباط نباشد اصلا امّا چون وصیّتها صاحب صناعت
در این باب حفظ کند و تربانی بتتبع آن وصایا میکند و عمل تمام شود

Akbar's cavalry

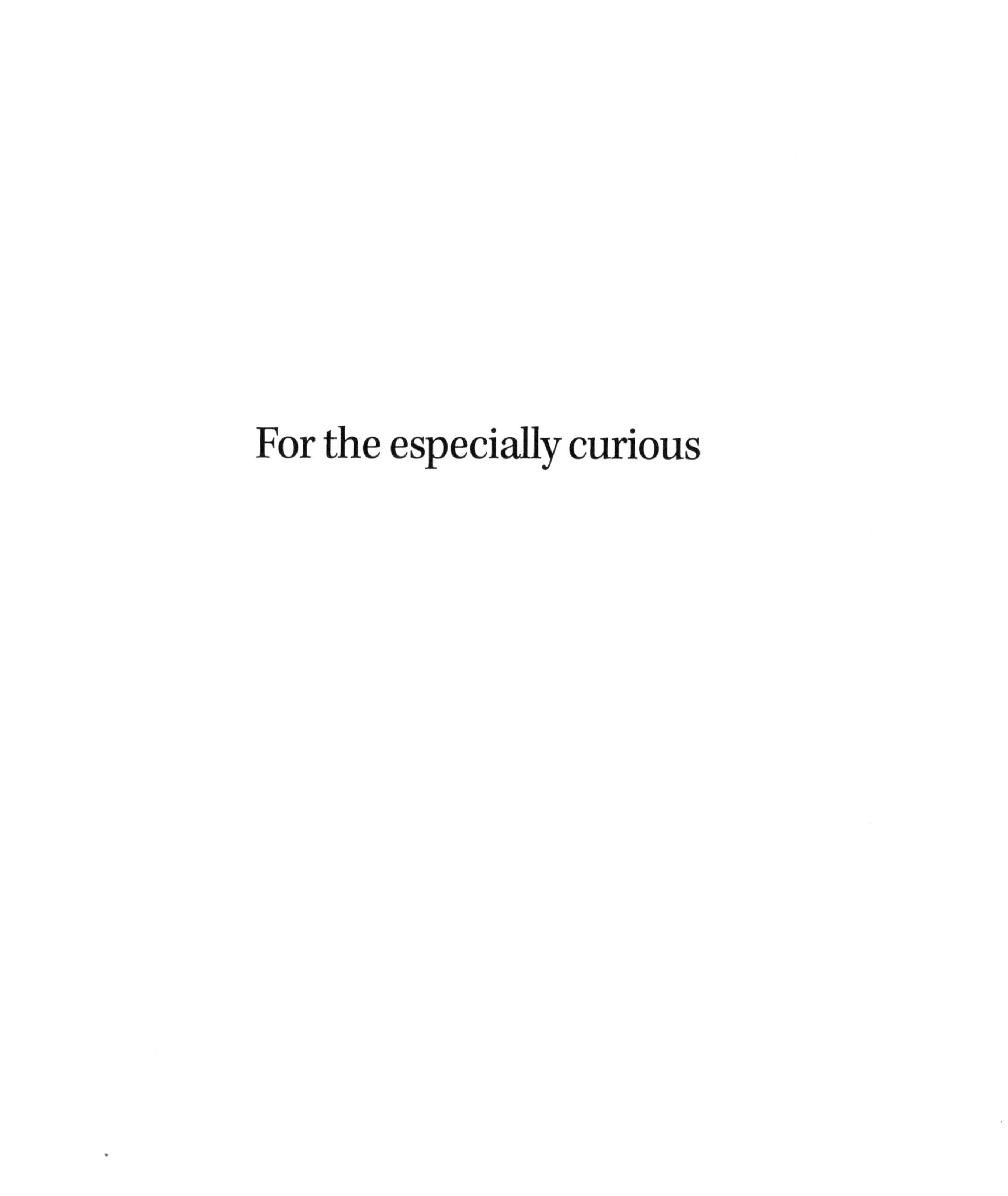

For the especially curious

1. A Difficult Beginning

Akbar's father, Humayun: Humayun came to India with his father, Babur, when he was seventeen years old. At the battle of Panipat, where guns were used for the first time in that part of India, he helped his father win a victory that gave him control of northern India. Babur was a very clever general who knew how to manage an army and keep control of an area once he had gained it. He also had a gentler side. He planted beautiful gardens wherever he went, wrote poetry, loved to have parties with his friends and wrote a book about his life in which he described the different plants and animals he had seen in India.

When Babur died at the age of forty-eight Humayun as the oldest son took over from him. He was much like his father in many ways. He was a great reader, always carried books with him, loved parties and visiting with his friends and took a great interest in the natural life of India, but he lacked his father's ability to command and organise. When ten years after his father's death a very able general named Sher Shah Suri challenged him he lost the battle and, as we know from the main story, had to leave India in a hurry taking only his family and a small army of friends with him.

Akbar and his mother: Humayun met Hamida, Akbar's mother, in his brother Hindal's camp during a party. He immediately announced to her family that he would like to marry her. Her mother and other women of the harem thought it was a good opportunity for her. "What could be better than to marry a king?" they asked her, but she told them that she thought she would be more comfortable marrying an ordinary person. She really didn't want to marry a king. Humayun sent for her to come and talk to him three times, but she always refused. It was only after forty days and much persuasion by the older members of the harem that she agreed to marry him.

Mughal carpets: As you can see from the miniature the floor of the palace in Kabul where Akbar joined his mother is covered with a beautiful carpet with flowers in bright shades of yellow, blue and red. When Akbar grew up and built his own palace he had many carpets designed and woven. He favoured animal designs featuring elephants, oxen, deer, lions, tigers, cheetahs and on one carpet a rhinoceros. The animals were always pictured in active poses: deer running, elephants prancing and tigers crouching for the spring. The colours were very bright with animals in a yellow beige or black against a strong red background.

A drummer: In this miniature you can see two parties going on, one inside and one outside of Humayun's palace in Kabul. In the miniature a low wall separates the two, but in real life the wall would have been very high, floor to ceiling, and thick so that the people on either side would not have been able to see or hear each other. On the street a band of horn players and kettle drummers, including the one shown opposite, is accompanying a sword dancer. Inside Akbar is celebrating with his mother and father surrounded by woman relatives, entertainers and servants.

The music inside would have been somewhat quiet and subdued making it possible for people to

carry on conversations, as you can see them doing. Outside with the use of the kettle drums and the horns the music would have been very loud.

A dancer: The dancers are adding greatly to the festivities. The dancer shown here is using castanets as are other members of the troop. If you look very closely at the miniature you will see a horn player providing the melody. The central dancer holds bells.

Refreshments: These two women are enjoying some refreshments. One has a glass in her hand and the other has a plate of food. Very likely the drink is sherbet, a very popular sweet drink flavoured with orange, lemon, pineapple or mango and served cold with ice brought in from the mountains and kept cold by storing it underground. The dessert may be a rice pudding, also very sweet,

tasting of ginger and cinnamon and full of almonds, raisins and pistachios.

Wall painting: There were many wall paintings in Mughal palaces, but very few of them have survived. Most have been painted over or faded with time. We know about them because people have described them in books, but also because, as here, they are painted into a miniature.

2. Growing Up

Akbar hunting: Royal children, both princes and princesses, learned to hunt, a difficult and somewhat dangerous sport. The children had to learn to keep their seat in the saddle while riding at full speed and managing a sword or shooting with a bow and arrows. A prince could in this way prove his skill and daring and show that when the time came he would become a brave and resourceful emperor.

A falconer: Falconry was a popular sport in the Mughal Empire. Birds of prey were trained to bring back their catches to their owners. As you can see in the picture Akbar's young friend is wearing a heavy leather glove to protect his hand from the bird's sharp claws. He is offering the falcon a piece of meat. The falcon will take the meat and forget all about the bird he has just caught, leaving the bird for the boy.

Falcon with prey: It took a great deal of patience to train a falcon. At first the owner had to take the bird around with him everywhere, talking softly to the bird and petting him gently until the bird became accustomed to him. Then while keeping the bird tied he used a lure (a stick with two bird wings attached), throwing it out and pulling it back over and over again, hour after hour, until the falcon learned to bring it back to him.

Once the bird had learned to do this the owner would let him free to hunt wild birds. It was very important that the owner kept in touch with the falcon at all times when they were hunting. He did this by shouting or whistling.

Water for the hunters: This young person is getting water from a little mountain stream in the hunting grounds. He is probably not one of the hunters but a royal servant who is taking care of the boys during the hunt.

A young archer: A bow and arrow was the main weapon used by the Mughals for hunting and for warfare. It was light and quick. A skilled archer could fire an arrow every five seconds and kill from a hundred metres. The young boys in the painting would not have been able to shoot like this, but they would have been working hard to improve their skills.

Two deer: Akbar's people, the Mughals, were great hunters. They hunted huge animals such as elephants (though these were not killed, but kept as working animals or pets). They hunted lions and tigers and killed them because they were seen as a danger to people. They hunted animals such as deer, wild boar, birds and rabbits for food.

A royal servant: This royal servant is rushing to assist the young boy who has caught the bird. He will carry the bird back to the royal kitchens where it will likely be prepared for the boys to eat that evening.

3. The Teenage Emperor

Akbar on Sky Rocket: In this miniature Akbar was riding a very dangerous elephant whose name was Sky Rocket. Of the 5,000 elephants kept in the royal stables he was considered to be the strongest and the most self willed. Elephants are generally peaceful animals except during the mating season when the males become restive and fight one another. Sky Rocket was in just such a state. With Akbar on his back he had been fighting on the royal sports field with a male elephant, Tiger in Battle, considered to be almost his equal. People standing about were at first amused as elephant fighting was considered a sport, but as the elephants grew more vicious they became concerned for Akbar and begged him to stop. They called for the Prime Minister to come and talk some sense into him. The Prime Minister arrived, took off his turban to express humility and pleaded with Akbar to stop, but Akbar ignored him.

Meanwhile the elephants took charge of the situation. Tiger in Battle decided he had had enough of the fight and broke away thundering out of the sports field and down the riverside path with Akbar on Sky Rocket in pursuit. Eventually they came to a pontoon bridge crossing the river. A pontoon bridge is not a very steady bridge. It is made up of small boats lashed together with a wooden plank surface laid over them. Elephants did cross on them but only one at a time walking very slowly. Tiger in Battle pounded onto the bridge and Sky Rocket followed. It was something of a miracle that Akbar and the two elephants made it across safely.

What the artist has done is to freeze a moment in time—a moment of extreme fear and concern, which you can see in the face and body language of everyone present. Even the river, normally painted peaceful and glassy is churned into agitation and if you look very closely, you will see a fish jumping into the air.

Akbar's face stands out in contrast. He is concentrating on the task in hand, getting his elephant under control.

Lifted boats: These boats have lifted and the men are working to push them back into place.

An argument: The men in this boat seem to be arguing about what is the best thing to do to help out in the situation.

The ferryman: This boatman by using a pole has ferried some rather important individuals carrying military standards across the river. He has seen the situation and appears to be pushing hard to get to the other side where he might be able to help.

A royal servant: According to observers a number of the royal servants plunged into the water in order to save Akbar if he fell in. If you look back at the miniature you will see that this one is attempting to shove a boat that has come loose back under the planking.

Gardeners: These men are very likely gardeners who were working in the garden behind the wall, heard the commotion and come rushing out to see if they can help.

A garden house: This is the only peaceful part of the picture. There were many gardens like this along the river. People in the little room at the top of the wall could see into the garden on one side and out onto the busy river on the other.

4. Fighting for the Empire

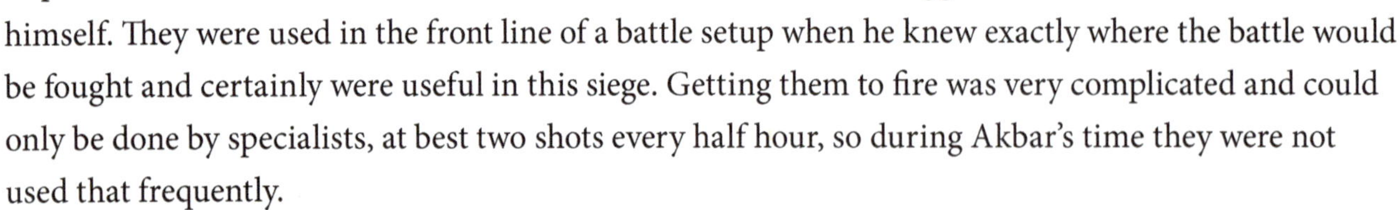

The big guns: Akbar was very proud of his big guns. He always had them placed near to his command tent where he could keep an eye on them. He was interested in any information he could gather about their use elsewhere and improvements that had been made to them and sometimes made suggestions himself. They were used in the front line of a battle setup when he knew exactly where the battle would be fought and certainly were useful in this siege. Getting them to fire was very complicated and could only be done by specialists, at best two shots every half hour, so during Akbar's time they were not used that frequently.

The cavalry: This very young soldier is a member of Akbar's cavalry, the most important part of his army. He is carrying a bow and arrows, as explained earlier, the major weapon used by the cavalry. The older soldier turning back toward him seems to be encouraging him as they climb up the hill to take possession of the city.

The tent city: As time went on Akbar developed a way of travelling with his army that was very comfortable—a tent city. It was put up anywhere he decided to stop for a while. Within the city he and his soldiers had a comfortable way to live. The streets were wide and orderly and lined with shops that sold products the soldiers were used to buying at home. Akbar had a large beautifully furnished tent that could serve as a meeting hall where government business could be discussed. If while he was on campaign he received letters telling of difficulties at home or in any other part of the empire he always had government ministers with him he could call together and have a discussion about how to handle the matter in a setting quite as dignified as at home.

Entrance to the city: This is a great moment for Akbar. He has just ridden up the pathway and entered a city that now belongs to him. He is speaking to Rao Surjan Singh, the former ruler of the city now surrendering the city to him.

Rao Surjan Singh : Rao Surjan Singh the commander of the fort is here surrendering to Akbar. It must have been very difficult for him at the time because we know from letters he wrote that his sympathies were very much for the Indian rulers he had served. Akbar invited him to his luxury tent in his tent city and offered him the title of Raja with command over fifty-two districts. He agreed and as far as we know became very satisfied working for Akbar.

This was Akbar's way with many of the people he conquered. Rather than punishing them for having fought against him he offered them good jobs in the new empire he was building up. He knew that as an outsider he could not just walk into a country and take it over. He had to somehow get the cooperation of the people who lived there.

The swords: Cavalry men carried swords for close encounters. The swords were very sharp and could split a person to the waist with one blow. Some of them were beautifully decorated with gold and precious stone inlays on the handle and the case. They can be seen in museums today where they are displayed as works of art.

The foot soldiers: Besides his specialist soldiers on horseback Akbar also had foot soldiers that fought in all of his big battles. These soldiers did not need the same specialist training as the cavalry and many of them came from the local population.

5. Making the Empire Work

Abd ur-Raham: As mentioned in the main story Akbar looks sad because he is talking to Abd ur-Raham, the four year old son of Bairam Kahn not long after the little boy's father was killed on his way to Mecca. As he promised, Akbar took him into his harem and acted like a father to him. Abd ur-Raham worked hard at his school work and became very clever at languages. By the time he grew up he could read and write in four different languages—Persian, Arabic, Turkish and Hindi. He is most famous for his poems in Hindi. He also worked as a commander of armies for Akbar, helping him gain control of Gujarat, Sind and the Deccan.

Akbar's nobles: The men shown here are nobles. Akbar appointed them and as long as they carried out his wishes and behaved honestly, they kept their jobs for life. In time of war it was their responsibility to provide him with a stated number of soldiers, horses and elephants with accompanying equipment. In time of peace they ruled different parts of the empire. They were paid very well in either money or income from lands they managed. Young men were always tying to attract Akbar's attention in the hope that he would appoint them as nobles.

Vina player: The vina was a stringed instrument that was plucked with a plectrum. If you look back at the miniature you will see that there are gourds hanging from the instrument. The gourds caused the sound to resonate. The vina produced a soft sound and was often used as background music for anything that was happening at court.

A lute player: This young man is carrying a plucked lute. He is standing just outside the court. He has raised his arm as though he is about to perform. He has no plectrum in his hand so it appears that this instrument is plucked with the fingers.

A pet cheetah: Cheetahs were pets in the Mughal Empire, very special pets. They were trained to work for their owners on the hunting grounds. Instead of shooting a deer with a gun or a bow and arrow the owner would release his cheetah and the cheetah would search for a deer, kill it and bring it back to the owner.

It took a very long time to train a cheetah to do this. First the cheetah had to be tamed. Once caught he would be kept blindfolded in a cage for a day or two until he became calmer. Then he would be fed with only the most tender cuts of meat: goat, deer, chicken or peacock. After he had become somewhat used to the system his trainer would appear while he was eating and speak to him in a low, soft, loving voice:" Come on, son, well done." The trainer would work with him for a long time until he had the cheetah's complete trust. The cheetah was considered tamed when he would lick butter from his trainer's hands. He then would be taken to the hunting grounds and taught to catch and bring back the prey.

Trained cheetahs were carried about in special ox carts with beautiful, brightly coloured carpets to rest on. Every evening they were taken for walks about the town. Some of them visited Akbar's court as you can see in the miniature

A royal horse: Horses were very much loved animals in the Mughal Empire. Akbar had 12,000 in his stables. His horses and most of the horses in the empire were used as war horses as described in the last chapter. Oxen and camels were the beasts of burden pulling carts or carrying goods on their backs. Even very wealthy people did not use horses to pull their carriages along the roads. They used very large beautiful white oxen. If you look closely at the miniature you will see that the horses visiting Akbar's court are decorated with feathers and yak tails as you saw in the miniature showing Mughal warfare.

Red headed falcon: People who owned falcons were very proud of them and took them about everywhere with them resting on their gloved hands.

6. Akbar's City

Splitting stone: Here we have pictures of two men with hammers. The first man is hammering in a spike to split a stone plank into facings for a brick wall. As mentioned in our main story the walls of the palace and the mosque were made of brick and then faced with red sandstone. The stone was taken from a quarry in a rough state and carried to a workplace outside the city where it was shaped into a plank. The finished plank was then brought to the building site to be cut into the exact size needed.

Carving a design: The second man is doing something quite different. He is cutting a design into a piece of stone that will be used for decoration on the walls. People who visit the city today as tourists are amazed to see the many beautiful designs cut into the red stone, some inlaid wih white marble.

A jali screen: This is a jali screen set into a window. Screens like this allowed light and air into a room, but protected people in the room from the strong Indian sunlight. The screens were very difficult to make. Using a specialist chisel a workman would carefully cut a design into a thin sheet of sandstone. He had to have a very steady hand. One mistake and the screen would be ruined.

An ox: As mentioned in the last chapter oxen were the main carriers of goods in the Mughal Empire. Where there were roads they pulled carts. If there were no roads and the land was rough they carried goods on their backs.

Room in the harem: This charming little room has whitewashed walls and a beautiful carpet, very much like the carpet in the first miniature in this book showing Akbar with his mother. There are jali screens around the sides of the room which would have allowed cooling breezes into the next rooms. Since this is a room in the harem it could very well have been for a royal prince or princess.

Making mortar: The two women in the miniature are making mortar—a mixture of sand, water and lime. The mortar was used to hold the bricks in the walls together and the stone facings to the wall. The woman shown here is beating up old bricks to create the sand. The other woman in the miniature is holding a basin of lime.

A porter: On Mughal building sites there were always men and quite often women carrying materials from one place to another. In this miniature you will find six porters, carrying bricks, mortar or materials to make mortar.

7. Akbar's Religion

Jesuit priests: These two Christian priests, Rudolf Aquaviva and Antonio Monserrate, had come from Europe to India at a time when it was very difficult and dangerous to travel. They had one objective in mind—to convert Indian people to Christianity. While staying in Goa, a city on the west coast of India, they were invited by Akbar to visit him and they were delighted. They hoped to convert him to Christianity with the expectation that following his example, many of his people would become Christians.

On their arrival they were further encouraged by Akbar, who asked to see them immediately. He had put on clothes with European touches and dressed his sons in similar costume to make them feel more comfortable. When they gave him a Christian Bible he took off his turban, put the Bible on his head and then kissed it to show his respect. He gave them a house in his palace and spent much time with them talking about the Christian religion. He took Antonio Monserrate on a lengthy military campaign to Kabul in order to have more time to talk with him. He was very fond of Rudolf Aquaviva and was seen walking about in his palace grounds in earnest conversation with him, his arm across the priest's shoulders. But in the end it became very clear to the priests that he had no intention of becoming a Christian and they asked to return to Goa.

Muslim clerics: Although the House of Worship was used for meetings with people of many different faiths on the occasion shown in the miniature there are only Christians and Muslims present. The topic under discussion is the "Word of God". The Muslims are willing to accept the Christian Bible as "a Word of God", but insist that the Koran is the final word. The Christians are saying that there is only one Word of God and that is in the Christian Bible. There is no agreement between the two groups and, as you can see, Akbar looks worried.

Akbar: From the very first the meetings in the House of Worship were a failure, even the meetings when only Muslims were present. He invited Sunnis, Shias and Sufis, people within the Muslim faith who had slightly different ideas, to come and talk together in the hope that they could resolve some of their differences. He was amazed when they ended up hurling insults such as "fool" and "heretic" at each other. Later, as we have seen, the situation only got worse when he brought in religious leaders from other faiths.

Eventually Akbar decided that he would make up his own religion and set about doing so. His religion contained many ideas of Islam, but included a law against the killing of animals, a belief of Hindus and Jains and encouraged the worship of the sun as practiced by Zoroastrians. His religion was not very popular. Only nineteen people joined and it was soon forgotten after his death.

Akbar's son, Salim: The two boys in the miniature are Akbar's sons, Salim and Murad. In the miniature they look patient, but not very interested. It must have been hard for them to stay up late at night to listen to religious discussions. Akbar was often a very demanding father. He felt that the boys had much to learn if they were to follow him in ruling the empire and he often treated them as though they were already grown up.

Child in street: This miniature shows an inside and outside scene. Inside the Christian priests and the Muslim clerics are having their discussion. Outside people are passing in the street. The little boy is a Hindu child out walking with his father. Because of the extreme heat in India, many native Hindus did not wear much clothing.

Muslim holy book: The book in the centre of the miniature is a Muslim holy book, which would have been written in a very beautiful Arabic script. It may very well be a Koran, the most important religious book of the Muslims. They believe It was dictated to Mohammed by the Angel Gabriel. It teaches people how to contact God through prayer and gives them rules to help them get along with one another. The Koran contains many of the same stories as those told in the Christian Bible.

Money bags: As explained in the chapter showing Akbar's court he liked to reward anyone he found to be doing good work. For this reason he always kept bags full of gold coins nearby. During his meeting in the House of Worship he gave out very little money because most of the religious people refused to listen to what others were saying and were very rude to anyone who did not agree with them.

8. The Workshop for Books

Student of calligraphy: Calligraphers were much revered in the Mughal Empire and in Akbar's workshop held a position above the artists. The written word was seen as the main vehicle for the transfer of ideas and therefore was considered to be more important than the pictures. Different calligraphers used different styles. There is a beautiful example of their work in the workshop miniature, a line of writing near the top and one near the bottom.

Teacher of calligraphy: There were many artists in Akbar's workshop, at one time over one hundred and they were always kept busy. As you will have noticed from looking at this book the miniatures were very detailed and complicated and would have taken a long time to paint. There were artists who spent an entire year on one painting.

The book the artists and calligraphers were working on in the miniature was called Nasir's Ethics. The book is about good ways for people to get along together in families and in communities. It was a great favourite of Akbar's and he often asked for it to be read to him. Many different books were produced in Akbar's workshops. There were books on astrology with paintings of the sky and books on the natural life of India with paintings of flowers, birds and animals. There were books on history, religion and philosophy and books about Akbar's life with pictures such a you have been looking at in this book.

Artist at work: There were also story books and when he was young Akbar especially liked these. Some of the stories were from Muslim countries and some were local Hindu stories. Akbar liked both. Two of Akbar's favourite stories were The Rama and The Hamza.

The Rama is the story of a Hindu god who is born as a person. He has many adventures on earth and at one point when his wife was stolen from him he was helped by the king of the monkeys and all his monkeys to get her back.

The Hamza is a story about an uncle of the Prophet Mohammed who believed in him when many other people were against him. He was very brave and fought in battles to protect Mohammed. After he died people began to tell stories about him and as they told them the stories became more and more fantastic, saying that Hamza travelled all over the world to convert people to the Muslim religion and had many adventures with sea monsters, wild animals and whole armies sent out to stop him. Most people knew the stories weren't true, but they loved them because they were lively and full of amazing events.

Artist with horse drawing: This artist has drawn a rearing horse. He very well may be illustrating an exciting adventure story.

Paper maker: This man is a paper maker. The paper was made from natural materials such as grass, the bark of trees and leaves of plants. To this old cotton or silk clothes were added. All the materials were cut into small pieces, moistened with water and pounded with a heavy hammer. The resulting pulp was put into a tank of water and caught on a screen made of woven grass. When dried the pulp became paper. The paper was then rubbed with a stone to make a good surface for the painters and calligraphers. The paper maker here is busy with this process.

The drinks table: From looking at the table you can see that drinks were the main refreshment provided for the workers. The weather in India is extremely hot and they would have needed to drink frequently. Some of the bottles may have held water, but others would have held sherbets, as described in the first chapter of this book, delicious fruit drinks. Ice from the mountains was delivered to Akbar's palace every day, so it would have been possible to keep the drinks cool.

Carved stone pillar: During his lifetime Akbar moved from one part of his empire to another. He stayed in Fatehpur Sikri, the city he built, for fifteen years, but then moved on to Lahore in the northern part of the empire. But wherever he was he arranged to have a workshop for books near his palace. He frequently visited the workshops to view the work of the artists and calligraphers and when he was particularly pleased with what they had done he would give them extra pay. The workshops were always beautifully built in carved stone like the one in the miniature.

Key to "Can you also find?"

Page 11. **Two swords**—dancer at bottom of painting. **A fly whisk**—top right hand side. **A dagger**—doorway bottom right. **Forest of trees**—top left. **Three containers of drinks**—right side, midway down. **Two horn players**—bottom left. **Two minarets**—top left.

Page 15. **Two swords**—*1,* top: boy with birds, *2,* mounted boy bottom right. **Two birds on a rock**—top left. **Four birds in flight**—right very top. **Yak tail decorations for horses**—all three horses. **A pink flower**—bottom left.

Page 19. **Eight bells** —on elephants. **A jumping fish** —top between the two boats . **A black feather** —on Akbar's hat. **Five cypress trees** —behind wall. **Two yak tail standards**—in midway boat. **Two open viewing platforms**—at top of wall.

Page 23. **Eight bushes**—three bushes on the left side just below the city wall and five on the hillsides to the upper right. **A dagger**—in the belt of the mounted horseman near centre. **Pita bread** —in city near gate. **A yak tail decoration**—on horse near three guns.

Page 27. **A bull**—lower left hand corner. **A fly whisk** —behind Akbar upper right. **A sword**—Akbar's belt. **Three daggers**—midway down, one right hand side, man in blue and two in belt of man very bottom centre. **Two yak tail decorations**—on horses, one in lower right hand corner and one midway down on left hand side. **A shield**—midway down on right side. **A white falcon**—bottom left side.

Page 31. **Akbar's secretary with pen and paper**—just below Akbar in dark maroon robe. **Two falcons** —in crowd just below Akbar. **Green ceramic tiles**—inner wall of roof garden. **A marble pool**—roof garden. **Two birds on a railing**—Inner wall of roof garden. **A tree on the side of a hill**—top of painting centre. **A keyhole doorway**—top left.

Page 35. **Thirteen books**—scattered about the room, some in the hands of the religious scholars and some on the floor. **A loaf of bread**—in the hands of a man on the street. **A tree**—at top of painting with stars and moon. **A dagger**—at Akbar's waist. **A yak tail**—on horse in street.

Page 39. **Four carpets with red flowers**—two at centre of painting and two at top. **An aqueduct**—top of painting. **Thirteen birds**—in sky at top of painting. **A pond**—at top of painting. **A flowering cherry tree**—bottom right of painting. **A channel of running water**—channel running across lower part of painting through pond.

For parents and teachers

This book grew out of an assisted reading programme I worked in at my local London school, North Harringay Primary School. The children I was tutoring did not have major problems but were held back by a reluctance to make the final effort that would bring them to a stage where reading comes easy and natural. The trick was to find them material that interested them so much they forgot they were reading.

The children in North Harringay come from different backgrounds, many of them Muslim. When I suggested that perhaps they would like to read about their country of origin I got an enthusiastic response. Over the years I discovered that the story of Akbar was the most compelling of all the cultures we read about. I particularly remember one boy, a "relectant reader" of the most determined sort, who when I told him I had found a book with a description of cheetahs at Akbar's court, snatched the book out of my hands and head bent over it, in the fiercest concentration, read a whole page. It was at that point I decided to write a book about Akbar.

The teachers at the school were very supportive of the project. The white boards in the classrooms made it possible to show the miniatures effectively to the whole class while one of my pupils pointed out various features. The response was good and further encouraged me to get to work on an Akbar book once I had retired.